CULHWCH AND OLWEN
CATHERINE FISHER

Culhwch and Olwen
Published in Great Britain in 2024
by Graffeg Limited.

Written by Catherine Fisher copyright © 2024.
Illustrated by Efa Lois copyright © 2024.
Designed and produced by Graffeg Limited
copyright © 2024.

Graffeg Limited, 24 Stradey Park Business Centre,
Mwrwg Road, Llangennech, Llanelli,
Carmarthenshire, SA14 8YP, Wales, UK.
Tel: 01554 824000. www.graffeg.com.

Catherine Fisher is hereby identified as the author
of this work in accordance with section 77 of the
Copyright, Designs and Patents Act 1988.

A CIP Catalogue record for this book is available from
the British Library.

All rights reserved. No part of this publication may
be reproduced, stored in a retrieval system or
transmitted, in any form or by any means, electronic,
mechanical, photocopying, recording or otherwise,
without the prior permission of the publishers.

The publisher acknowledges the financial support of
the Books Council of Wales. www.gwales.com.

ISBN 9781802586459

1 2 3 4 5 6 7 8 9

CULHWCH AND OLWEN
CATHERINE FISHER

ILLUSTRATIONS BY EFA LOIS

Cadno

1. How Culhwch was Born

It begins with Daylight.
It begins with Goleuddydd.

She lay curled in the mud and the leaves and the berries. Her hands clutched acorns. Pain pulsed through her body.

Far above, through the branches of a great hollow oak, she could see the sky, high and blue, and the sun, sending down shafts of light.

Her name was all she had left. There was nothing else in her memory, no knowledge of who she was or where she had come from, or how she had crept here, to the depths of this tanglewood.

She sat up. Every moment was a stiffness and an ache, and she was shivering with cold. How long had she wandered in the forest? Now she could see that her dress of velvet and gold was tattered and ruined, that her delicate white arms were scratched by brambles. She was a lady, she was sure of it, a king's daughter and a woman of quality. Why was she here?

Propped on her palms, the acorns and dead leaves wet beneath her, she listened. She heard a new sound.

Not the wind in the leaves.

Not the whistle and click of small birds.

Something stranger.

Something warm and wet, something snorty and squealish.

Suddenly, between the trees, she saw animals, large white snouted creatures, each with one red ear, and she stared at them in astonishment, because she had no idea what they were.

The pain came again. She put back her head and screamed.

The scream rang through the forest. It echoed down aisles of oaks, into hollows of birch and thickets of holly, up hillsides and hidden streams. It echoed deep in a valley of golden beech trees where a prince pulled his horse to a standstill and turned his head, startled.

"Did you hear that?" His men listened. "It's her! It's my wife!"

He spurred on, the grey cloaked riders racing after him through the wildwood. He was burning with fear. He was icy with dread.

"Lady?"

A face was close up to hers, a red, sunburned face, worn by weather, its eyes deep in wrinkles. "Lord bless us, lady, you shouldn't be here. Not in your condition. Are you

Prince Cilydd's wife? He's been searching for you for weeks now. Let me help you."

Goleuddydd stared at him, and beyond him, at the white pigs snorting and grunting for acorns in the litter.

Her mind cleared. "Cilydd..." she whispered.

"Yes." The swineherd knelt awkwardly and helped her up. "And God knows what his wrath and relief will be when he sees the state of you. My shelter is near here. It's not much, just a brushwood covering, but it's something, though not where you should be. You should be safe and warm in a palace, lady, with your women around you, not lying here in the rain.. This is no place for a prince to be born."

She nodded, and struggled up. It was hard to walk. Her belly was stretched and swollen; it impeded her and weighed her down. He led her to a hovel of woven branches, its floor mucky straw. She crumpled, grateful to have no rain falling in her eyes.

Her dress was sodden. Her fingers dripped water. "My name is Goleuddydd," she whispered.

"I know, my lady."

She looked at her nails, dirty and broken. "How long have I been in this wilderness?"

"Weeks. I heard at Lammas that a madness came down on you. It happens sometimes, they say..." He bustled, lighting a fire and turning to fetch water in a leather bucket. "There is no rhyme or reason to it. My own mother had a turn like that once, but..."

The pain.

It went through her like a knife and she screamed till she could breathe again.

"Don't worry. The baby's coming," the swineherd said. He pulled a face and shook his head. "I've delivered many a piglet, but never a prince. Mary and the angels guard us..."

She barely heard him. Because the life inside her was pushing its way out.

Cilydd flung himself from his horse and plunged into the brambled undergrowth. "It was near here! Hurry!"

The second scream had split his fear into two, for Goleuddydd, and the child.

Nettles whipped his hand; he crashed down a muddy slope and into a small stream. Water up to his knees, he waded across and scrambled up the trampled bank. Then one of his men yelled. "Look! Smoke!"

The baby came.

He came with a squalling and an eager cry, into the rain and the wind. He came like a hero, without fear. He yelled aloud his triumph.

The swineherd wrapped him hastily in his own ragged coat. He looked down into the small, puckered face. "Well,

well, he's a lively lad! A lusty fellow, lady."

She nodded.

She was pale and tired.

He didn't like the look of her.

At that moment the pigs erupted into squeals and fled like white streaks into the wood. Suddenly there were men everywhere, tall men with glittering swords and tunics of saffron and cloaks of cloth-of-gold and scarlet, and they pushed the swineherd aside and snatched the child from him. The lord Cilydd looked down at the shining face of his son. Then he sat weakly by his wife's side.

"I thought I was too late," he gasped.

"You are too late, my lord." She breathed slowly, and her hand was white as it held his. "I was lost before, and now I will be lost to you again."

"Goleuddydd. Don't say that…"

"I don't know where I have been. Down wild ways, along forgotten paths. Maybe not even in this world! All I remember is sitting by the fire on Lammas night and then, for no reason, standing up and going to the door and looking out. It was cold and windy. Something was calling to me. I wanted to turn away, but I couldn't. I stepped outside. What is it out there in the wild and the wilderness that calls us like that?"

"Don't you remember anything?"

"Nothing. Until now."

"We searched for weeks. You were nowhere..."

"That is exactly where I was. But it's over now." Her fingers closed on his. "I don't have much time left, so listen to me. The boy is to be called Culhwch."

"*Pig-run?* But..."

"It will be his name. The boar is a sacred animal for him. It will shape his destiny. Come closer."

He bent. Her breath was the softest warmth on his cheek. She smelt of wood and briar and wildness. She whispered, "I will die of this birth, it is happening now. You will want to marry again..."

"NO! No, I..."

She shook her tangled hair. "Men are weak, women decide these things. Marry and be happy if you want to, but not until my son is tall. Not until you see a two-headed bramble growing on my grave."

"But..."

"Promise me!"

He nodded his head.

"Now," she whispered, "bring me the priest."

The priest was fetched – a small humble man who hurried from his horse. He brought out his cross and his holy water and his book, but before he could say a word she had hold of his hand and her grip was like iron and her voice a whisper. "I lay this dying command on you. Every year you will clear my grave. Nothing must grow on it. No weed, no bramble. Nothing! Do you understand?"

Astonished, the priest nodded.

Then he began the words of the Sacrament, as Cilydd stood above with the child in his arms.

Before the words were ended, she was gone.

2. The Priest Tends the Grave

At first the ground is lumpen. Ragged grass, cracked mud.
No need to weed this mess.

Years pass. Dock and thistle sprout.
He brings a spade and digs them out.

He's busy. Gets there late on an autumn evening.
There are shoots. On his neck her angry breathing.

A decade of dandelion, nettle-sting.
He has grey hair now. His hands, uprooting.

Who can stop this green life? It just comes.
A dead queen torments his dreams.

Boys play on the graveyard wall. His knees hurt.
Thorns tangle around his heart.

He'll be as cold as her next winter.
Every tale has another chapter.

3. Culhwch Hears his Destiny

Culhwch waited in the hall. He felt uneasy and breathless. He wore his finest tunic and cloak and his gold-hilted sword.

Two months ago his father had been out hunting and Culhwch had been with him, and they had ridden, as they always did, past the churchyard where his mother was buried.

Cilydd had glanced down at her grave. Then, with a hiss of wonder, he had leapt down from his horse and walked over to the grey unhewn stone.

"What is it?" Culhwch let his horse circle and stamp. His father had knelt on the bare earth where nothing ever grew. When he had spoken his voice was raw with wonder. "A sign. At last!"

From the grave a two-headed briar was growing. It was thorny and had tangled round on itself; spiders' webs hung from it, glistening with rain. Fat blackberries clustered among its brambles.

Culhwch knew that the old priest who had been his

mother's chaplain had died only a month ago. Certainly, this was no coincidence.

His father wasted no time. "I want a new wife."

"King Doged has a daughter," his men told him. "She would be just right for you."

It was as if they had been planning it for years, just waiting, chafing, eager as dogs. That night the warband saddled and bridled; they gathered their weapons and rode out into the dark and the winter mist.

Culhwch had waited at home, with the children and the old people and the bards. Next morning, the men returned. They brought gold and horses and hounds. They drove a hundred red cattle before them. Women walked behind them, weeping and sorrowful.

His father led a white horse and on its back was a woman dark of hair and angry of eyes. Fury burned in her. Her anger scared Culhwch; he could not hate her for it, but he knew it was deep and most dangerous to him.

Today, in the church, his father had married the woman, King Doged's daughter. When they asked her name all she would say was "Tywyllwch."

Which means Darkness.

Now, standing at the door of the hall, Culhwch watched as his father and his new wife came into the warmth and the crowd. A great cheer went up, men waved their ale-cups, dogs barked, women applauded, bards tuned their harps.

Prince Cilydd smiled around at his warband, and then he led the woman to her throne, and she sat and looked at her new tribe with dark, bitter eyes.

She wore a robe of deepest purple, and armlets of curled bronze. Her neck-torque was heavy gold, in the form of curling serpents. She was a strong, powerful woman.

And Culhwch could feel her anger; it coiled round her like the snakes, it burned her like the flames of the fire. She had been stolen from her home, and her husband had been killed. Now she burned for revenge.

She stood up.

"Do you have children, my lord? Have I come to a childless house?"

"Not at all!" Cilydd said. He took Culhwch's arm and pulled him forward to the table. "See lady, this is my son. A fine boy. As handsome as me!"

Everyone laughed.

The dark queen did not laugh. She looked at Culhwch and he looked at her. He tried not to show fear, but maybe she saw deep into him, because she smiled, and she said, "Well. He's a grown boy. It's time he was married. He will marry who I choose."

Culhwch shivered. He said quickly. "No."

"What did you say?"

"I said 'No'. I want to choose my own wife..."

The new queen smiled, as if she had been waiting for

that word. "NO? What a disobedient boy, a wilful boy! So now listen to me, boy born in a pig-run, while I lay this curse on you." And before anyone could move, before any druid could speak or warrior stop her, she raised her hand and pointed one finger at him. "This is my saying. You will never have a wife, ever, in all your life, unless you marry Olwen, the daughter of Ysbaddaden, Chief of Giants."

The people gasped. They cried out in horror.

Cilydd crumpled onto a chair. Culhwch stood frozen in despair.

Ysbaddaden! Chief of Giants!
A name from lost tales.
So enormous he could barely stand.
And if he did his head was high among the clouds!
His eyelids so heavy they had to be propped up on forked sticks by his servants! His appetite so vast that he ate men for breakfast, dinner and supper!
So what must his daughter be like?

And yet, deep inside Culhwch's heart a flame sprang into fire.
Olwen.
The name left small white prints in his heart.
Prince Cilydd stood heavily. He knew there was nothing he could do against such a terrible and bitterly spoken

curse. He said, "My son, you have heard your destiny. I have only one piece of advice for you. Ride at once to the court of your cousin, Arthur. He has many marvellous men. He can help you in this quest, if you approach him in the right way. "

"How do I do that?" Culhwch asked, anxiously.

His father smiled. "Easy. When you get there, ask him to trim your hair."

4. How Culhwch Rode Out

On a steed four winters old, grey-headed, well-striding, hooves like shell, a gold bridle in its mouth.

A precious gold saddle under him.
Two sharp spears of silver in his hand.

A battle-axe, arm-long, that draws blood from the wind, and strikes faster than a dew-drop falls.

A gold-hilted sword belted on his thigh.
A gold shield, lightning-flash, on his back.

Two spotted, white-chested greyhounds collared with red gold running round him, left-right, right-left.

His steed's hooves slicing the soil so it flew up round his head like four swallows.

A purple, four-cornered cloak about him,
a ball of gold on each corner, every ball worth a thousand cows.

So light the canter, so smooth the gallop
not a tip of Culhwch's golden hair was stirred

till he came to the gate of Arthur's court.

5. Culhwch Enters the Court of Arthur

"Is there a gatekeeper?" Culhwch demanded.

A large man got up from a bench by the gate. He folded his arms.

"There is, and it's me. I'm Glewlwyd Great-Grip, Arthur's Chief Gatekeeper. I only work on every first of January, which is today. I have deputies for all the other days."

"Open the gate."

"I won't."

"Why not?"

"Because knife has gone into meat, and drink into horn, and there's a crowd in Arthur's court. The feast has started; unless you're a king or a craftsman, you're not allowed in." Glewlwyd grinned. "But don't worry, princeling, you'll be looked after.

"You'll have food for your dogs and horse, hot spicy meat for yourself, and wine and songs in that hostel over there with all the other visitors, and a good bed for the night. And tomorrow, when the gates are opened, you can go in first, and sit wherever you like in Arthur's hall."

Culhwch was dismayed. He had ridden a long way and he was tired and hungry and a bit scared. He decided to be bold.

"That's not good enough, "he snapped. "If you don't open this gate I'll bring dishonour on this court. I'll raise three shouts that will be heard from Cornwall to Ireland. And all the women who hear it will be so scared that their babies will be born too early."

Glewlwyd was astonished. "You can shout as much as you want, but you're not going anywhere until I go and speak with Arthur."

"Well go on then," said Culhwch. "And hurry up."

The gatekeeper went into the hall and pushed his way through the noise and merriment of the feast until he came to the high table where Arthur sat with his wife Gwenhwyfar and his closest warriors, Cai and Bedwyr. Arthur looked up and said, "What's the news from the gate?"

Glewlwyd folded his arms. He said:

Two thirds of my life have gone, and two thirds of yours.
I've been in Caer Se and Asse. In Sach and Salach.
In Lotor and Ffotor. I was in India.
I was in the battle of the two Ynyrs when twelve

hostages were taken from Norway. I've been in Europe, in Africa, in Corsica.
I was there when you defeated the warband of Gleis,
When you killed Mil the Black,
When you conquered the land of Greece.
I was with you in the fortresses of Oeth and of Anoeth
And the castle of Nefenhyr Nine-Teeth.
We've seen a lot of strong, kingly men in our time, Arthur. But never in all my life have I seen a man as handsome as the one at your gate this minute."

Arthur was astonished. "Well if you walked in then run out, and let him in. It's a shameful thing for such a man to be left out in the wind and rain."

Cai turned his head. He was Arthur's foster brother. He said softly, "Why break the laws of the court for a stranger?"

Arthur shrugged. "We're only noblemen as long as others seek us out. The more generous we are, the more our honour and fame will grow, brother."

They both waited.

Everyone looked towards the door.

When Glewlwyd opened the gate for him Culhwch rode straight in. He trotted his horse right inside the great hall,

and all the warriors and women and bards and druids and priests stared in astonishment, because they had never seen a prince so handsome or so superb a steed.

Culhwch sat calmly in the saddle. He said, "Hail, Arthur, chief of the kings of the Island of the Mighty! I greet you and all your warband, every one of you. I wish you all honour and grace."

"Greeting to you too, Prince," Arthur stood. "Come and sit at my table, among my men, and share our food and songs."

Culhwch shook his head. "I haven't come here for food and drink. But there is a gift I do want."

Arthur said, "Though I don't know you, you can have any gift I can give, as far as the wind dries, as far as the rain falls, as far as the sun shines, as far as the sea spreads, and as far as the ends of the earth. Except, that is, for my ship, my cloak, my sword, my spear, my dagger..."

Gwenhwyfar glared at him. "... And my wife."

"Really?" Culhwch asked.

"God's truth. Name it."

Culhwch took a breath, then he said, "First I want to have my hair trimmed. By your own hand."

The Court murmured in surprise.

Arthur was still a moment. He turned and made a sign; a servant brought an ebony comb and silver shears.

Culhwch climbed down from his horse, and gave the

reins to a servant. Arthur stood up, combed the boy's hair, and snipped the golden ends.

As he did so he shivered and stepped back, because he knew instantly that this man was related to him. "Who are you?" he gasped. "I feel such a strange warmth towards you; we must be of the same blood."

"We are. My name is Culhwch. I'm the son of Cilydd son of Celyddon Wledig."

"Then you're my cousin!" Arthur threw down the comb and hugged him. "So you deserve a huge welcome gift. Tell me what it is, and it's yours!"

Culhwch looked round at the hundreds of warriors and women. He felt very scared. But he spoke up boldly enough.

"I want Olwen, the Giant's daughter, for my wife. And I ask for her in the name of all your magical men and women."

6. Arthur's Magical Court

*Culhwch asked for his gift
in the names of Arthur's men.
Cai first, then Bedwyr.
Gwrhyr All-Tongues
and kind Gwalchmai.
Sgilti and Taliesin,
and Gwyn ap Nudd.
Osla Big-Knife,
Gilla the Leaper.
Bards, druids, priests,
the women of the Court,
warriors and champions,
sorcerers, magicians, scullions,
rogues, villains, kings and demons.
Names from ancient tales,
names from dreams,
the whole crazy crowd,
the ferocious host,
two hundred witnesses.
Culhwch named them all.*

7. Cai the Fair

Arthur listened in silence. Then he said, "Well, prince, I've never heard of this girl, but I'll send out messengers to find her for you. It may take some time."

Culhwch nodded.

"In the meantime you are my guest."

Arthur summoned a whole host of messengers and sent them out at once on the search for Olwen. They travelled right across the Island of the Mighty, through valleys, forests and mountain ranges. Some crossed the sea in ships and searched to the far ends of the earth. It took a year for them all to come back again, but at the end of the search not one of them had any news of the Giant or his daughter.

Culhwch shook his head in bitter disappointment. "This is bad. I came to you because your Court is the greatest. Now I will have to leave and tell everyone you've failed, and that Arthur's men are not as powerful as everyone thinks."

The Court went silent. Arthur looked devastated. Nobody could say a word.

Until Cai turned his head. "Ah, Prince," he said in his

soft, dangerous voice, "you must not insult Arthur like that." For a moment Culhwch was scared. But then Cai smiled his cold smile. "I'll tell you what we'll do. We'll set out together, you and I, and I will find you this girl. Because if I can't find her, she doesn't exist."

Cai stood up.

Cai the fair.
Cai the clever.
The handsomest man
in Arthur's court.
Can hold his breath under water
for nine days and nights.
For nine days and nights
can go without sleep.
A slash from his sword
no doctor can heal.
Can grow tall
As a tree in the forest.
What he holds in his hands
never gets wet.
What he holds in his hands
can never be seen.
Fire in his fingers
never goes out.
Cold hands, cold heart.

Sinister-swift.
There's no one like Cai
in the wide world!

Arthur chose some men with special powers to go with Cai and Culhwch. He called on Bedwyr to join them, because although Bedwyr only had one hand (the other was of silver) his spear thrust was ferocious. Cynddylig the Guide had to go because he could always find out ways and roads, even in the wildest landscape. Gwrhyr All-Tongues had the gift of being able to speak every language, including those of animals and birds, so he would be useful. Menw the sorcerer was chosen because if they needed it he could cast a spell that would make them all invisible. Last of all, Arthur chose his nephew, the famous Gwalchmai, his best man on a horse, best man on foot. He never returned home without completing the quest he had set out for.

Culhwch was delighted with these companions. Now, he thought, surely he would be able to find the Giant's daughter!

8. The Biggest Fortress in the World

They set out, and travelled for a long time through the wizened woods and winding ways of Wales. Finally, on a cold winter's afternoon, they came down from the hills onto a great plain of grass, and far in the distance they could see a fortress, high against the sky.

They stopped and stared at it.

"It's enormous," Culhwch whispered.

Cai nodded. The others shifted uneasily in their saddles. It had to be the biggest fortress in the world.

"Come on," Cai said. "Not far now."

But when they set out towards it, something strange happened. They rode all day until darkness came down, and the fortress was no nearer than before.

Cai frowned. "There's magic in this."

The next day, and the day after, the same thing happened. However far and fast they rode, the fort stayed the same distance away. Finally Cai stopped, furious.

He glared at Menw. "Do something!"

Menw was ready. He dismounted and spoke salty

magic words and conjured with air and earth and water and fire.

Then he climbed back on his horse. "Try now," he said, smug.

This time, when they rode, the fortress grew nearer. Cai grinned, but Culhwch felt nervous.

When they came up to the vast black walls they saw that all the meadows around were crowded with sheep – a bleating, baaing sea of wool. There was a shepherd looking after the flock, standing on a mound. He had a furry dog with him, as big as a horse. As they watched, the dog breathed out a fiery breath, and shrivelled a tree. All over the plain, it had burned every tree and bush to the ground.

The shepherd watched them come.

Cai said, "Gwrhyr All-tongues, go and talk to that man. Find out who lives in the fort. It seems to me this is the place we've been looking for."

Gwrhyr was usually as brave as anyone. But now he shook his head. "Only if you come with me, Cai. That dog...!"

"Don't worry about the dog," Menw said quietly. "I'll cast a spell to make him sleep. He won't harm you."

Sure enough, a few moments later the dog lay down and began to snore loudly. Cai and Gwrhyr rode up to the shepherd. Cai said, "Greetings! There are a lot of sheep here. You must be very rich."

"They're not my sheep, strangers. I'm just the shepherd." The man scowled, and it was true, he wore only rags and skins. "I was a lot richer once."

"What happened?" Cai said softly.

"My wife Elin happened. The Giant wanted to marry her, but she refused him, and now he's taken everything we own. Not only that, she's jealous! She watches everything I do in case other women chase me."

Gwrhyr choked back a laugh.

Cai smiled. "So whose sheep are they?"

"Are you stupid! Whose do you think? They belong to HIM. Ysbaddaden Chief-Giant. That's his fortress over there. All the sheep, all the cows, all the woods, all the crops are his. Every fool in the world knows that."

By this time, the others had come closer and were listening. Culhwch felt a shiver of excitement. They had found the right place! He asked, "What's your name, shepherd?"

"My name's Custennin. Ysbaddaden is my brother, though he's grown so huge and monstrous and swollen I barely recognize him these days. He took all my money away, he killed twenty-two of my sons, and now he makes me slave for him. Anyway, who are you, asking all these nosy questions, and why are you here?"

"Sir, we're messengers from Arthur," Gwalchmai said, in his courteous way. "We are searching for Olwen, the

Giant's daughter. This young man wishes to marry her."

"WHAT!" The shepherd looked terrified. "Are you mad? Take my advice, turn around and go home. Right now! No one gets out of that fortress alive!"

The shepherd nudged his dog but before it could wake Culhwch said, "Wait!"

He took a small gold ring from his finger and gave it to the shepherd. "Take this."

"What for?"

"As my gift."

The shepherd stared at the ring as it lay in his big dirty palm. He tried to slide it on his smallest finger, but it was still too tiny so he dropped it into his glove for safety. "Thanks," he said gruffly. "Well, I'm going now. Sorry I couldn't help, but take my warning seriously. Turn around and get right away from here."

He whistled and the huge sleepy dog drove the sheep off towards the castle. Cai glanced at Culhwch. "Very clever," he said.

Culhwch felt proud to be praised by Cai. "If it works."

Cai smiled, and watched the shepherd and his sheep cross the plain. "Oh, it will work. If his wife is as jealous as he says she is."

9. The Twisted Log

Custennin the shepherd was late home for supper.

He penned the sheep and ducked under the low doorway of his thatched house. The smell of stew rose to greet him – onions and carrots and beef. His mouth watered. "Take those mucky clothes off first," his wife said.

She brought the stew to the table and the shepherd was so eager for it he dumped his gloves and hat in her arms and sat down at once. But before his spoon got to his mouth she said, "What's this?"

The shepherd looked up and closed his eyes in dismay.

His wife had the gold ring in her hand.

Elin was a strong, fierce woman. She always seemed a bit angry at him. Now she looked furious. "Where did you get this?"

He was so scared his spoon rattled and foolishly, he made up the first thing that came into his head. "I... er... I went fishing. Down by the sea. And er... I saw something shiny washed in by the tide. And um, I saw it was a ring..."

Elin snorted in disbelief. "Absolute nonsense! You got it from some woman."

"NO! It was..."

"Tell me the truth! Or I'll tell the Giant you're keeping treasure from him."

The shepherd sighed. "You wouldn't do that. But all right. It's nothing to get excited about. The ring was a gift from a young prince. He's out there with his companions, and his name is Culhwch, son of Cilydd. He's come here because he wants – can you believe it! – to marry Olwen."

Elin's eyes widened. She felt a great shock of delight, and then another one of sadness. She loved Olwen, and it would be wonderful if this young prince could marry the girl, and take her away from her dreadful father. But the Giant was so sly and dangerous! Everyone else who had tried it was dead.

She tossed the ring in a drawer. "Put down that spoon at once and go and get those men in here. I want to see them. NOW!"

He took another big gulp and then hurried out. While she waited she paced anxiously up and down, until she heard the clink of harness and the voices of men and ran quickly outside.

Arthur's men!

She raced up and was so eager to embrace them that she threw herself at Cai with her arms wide.

Cai took one look and thought fast. He snatched a big log up from the woodpile and thrust it into her arms and she hugged it so tight it was bent into a twisted spiral.

Cai stared at it, appalled. "Woman," he said. "If that had been me I'd never have hugged anyone any more! You have a powerful sort of embrace!"

Elin laughed. "Sorry. It's just that I'm so glad you've come!"

They all went into the house and were served with stew and meat. And while they were eating a strange thing happened, because Elin went to a large metal chest that stood at one end of the chimney hearth and she opened it and said, "Come out and have some food now."

The men were astonished when a boy with yellow curly hair climbed out of the chest and stretched his cramped arms and legs. He fell on the food as if he was starving, and gobbled it down.

"Who's this?" Gwalchmai asked. "And why is he hidden? Not as a punishment, surely?"

Elin sighed. "This is the last of our sons. The Giant killed his twenty-two brothers. He is all we have left. So now we hide him to try and keep him safe but..." she shook her head in despair. "I dare not think what will happen if Ysbaddaden finds out."

Cai looked at the boy. "What's his name?"

"He's the last of our sons, and the best," his father said. "So we call him Goreu which means Best."

Cai nodded. "Then let him come with me, and join my companions. We'll look after him and teach him a few things."

Goreu was overjoyed, and they all ate a hearty meal. But at the end of it Cai laid down his knife and said, "Now. We want to see this girl Olwen. Does she ever come out of that fortress?"

Elin nodded. "She comes to see me every week when she washes her hair in the stream. She leaves her rings in a bowl and never takes them away, so that we have some gold to spend. Such a lovely girl."

"Will she come now if you send her a message?"

Elin looked at him suspiciously. "No harm will come to her?"

"None."

"Are you sure? I want your word, stranger."

Cai nodded. "I give you my word as Arthur's warrior. She will be unharmed. I swear it."

The message was sent. And Olwen came.

10. OLWEN

She wore a robe of flame red silk.
A necklace of red gold about her neck.
Precious pearls, shining jewels.
Her hair was yellower than the flowers of the gorse.
Her skin was whiter than the foam on the sea.
Her hands and her fingers were delicate
As cottongrass in a bubbling stream.
Her eyes glinted
Like the eyes of a tamed hawk,
Like the eyes of a mewed falcon.
No eyes were brighter than hers.
Her neck was purer than a swan's.
Her cheeks were redder than a foxglove.
Everyone who saw her loved her at once.

Four white clovers grew up where she stepped.
That's why they called her Olwen.

As she came into the dark thatched house Culhwch rose and they stood face to face. And in that moment they loved each other with a love that was fierce and true.
    Everyone else watched in silence.

Culhwch took Olwen's hand. He said, "I have loved you since I first heard your name. Will you come away with me now, to Arthur's Court?"

Olwen shook her head. She looked at him and her gaze was clear. "I do choose you for my husband. But it won't be that easy. My father has made me give my word that I would never run away without telling him. The reason is that he is under a curse. When I take a husband, the Giant will die. So of course he will try to kill you."

"But..."

Olwen shook her head, proud and firm. "Don't ask me to break my word. I will never do that." She looked round, at Cai and Gwalchmai and the others. "But don't worry. You have brave companions, and I have a plan."

They sat around the table. Culhwch could not take his eyes off the girl; she was so beautiful, and brave. He felt as if he had known her for ever.

"This is what you have to do," Olwen said. "First, enter the fortress. You'll find there are nine gatekeepers, all fierce, armed men, and nine terrible wolfhounds. You will have to get past them all."

"No problem," Cai said darkly.

"Then you must go through the corridors into the heart of the castle. In the very central hall you will find my father the Giant. He is so enormous that the ceiling is as high as the sky. You must tell him you want to marry me.

You'll have to do this three times because each time he will make some excuse, and each time he will try to kill you, so be ready."

Culhwch nodded. "We will."

"Then, on the third time you ask, he'll give you a list of tasks – of things and people you have to find for him. The list will seem impossible and endless, but for everything he demands, just answer carelessly, "Yes, that will be easy for us." Never show any doubt or fear. Act as if it was all nothing. If you show even a flicker of fear, he will kill you all."

Culhwch frowned. He wondered if he would be able to stand before the enormous Giant and show not even a scrap of fear. Surely his voice would tremble and his hands shake?

"I'll try," he said firmly.

Olwen stood up. "I believe you," she whispered.

Then she turned and ducked under the low door, and it seemed to Culhwch as if the light went out with her.

Only a trail of white flowers showed where she had been.

11. Forks Under his Eyelids

"Right." Cai drew his sword. "Are we ready?"

They all nodded. All six companions were there, and the yellow-haired boy, Goreu, was with them.

"Let's go!"

They charged into the fortress.

The fight with the nine gatekeepers and their wolfhounds didn't take long. Cai was fast and fierce and in no mood to waste time. He cut his way through and the others followed him, leaving a heap of groaning men and whimpering dogs behind them.

They followed a trail of white flowers down dank corridors and through stony chambers, under cobwebbed archways and through crooked doors, until they came into the vastest hall any of them had ever seen.

In the middle of it, sitting on a throne of stone, was Ysbaddaden Chief-Giant.

There is no description of the Giant.
How could there be?

He's too huge, too terrible.
There are no words that fit him.
No sentence big enough.
He takes your breath away.
He freezes you with fear.
Everything you're scared of,
Every shiver of dread,
Every crawl of your skin
Is there, in that chair.

To defeat him
You'll need everything you are.

Culhwch stood frozen in terror.

But Cai shouted, "Greetings, Ysbaddaden, from Arthur's men."

"Why are you here?" the Giant demanded. His voice was a rumble in the stone vault of the roof.

"We're here to ask for the hand of your daughter Olwen, to marry this young prince, Culhwch son of Cilydd."

The Giant roared. "WHAT! Where are my useless servants and rascals!! Lift up my eyelids so I can see this fool who wants to be my son-in-law!"

His servants came running, carrying long forked sticks. With a great effort they propped them under the Giant's enormously heavy eyelids and heaved them up, until his red eyes glared out like setting suns. "Where is he?"

Culhwch stepped forward.

"So that's what you look like! And you want to marry my daughter?"

"I love her," Culwhch said boldly.

"Oh you do, do you? *Well this is my answer.*"

The Giant snatched one of the three poisoned spears that he kept ready by his throne, and threw it at Culhwch.

Quick as a flash Bedwyr caught it and flung it back. It stuck in the Giant's kneecap.

"OUCH!" the Giant roared. "That stings! Now I'll limp when I walk downstairs. Curse you and that spear and whoever made it! Servants! Raise my eyelids higher, so I can see these strangers better!"

The servants gasped and forced the forked sticks up a little higher. Now the Giant's eyes were as red as the rising sun.

Cai folded his arms. "That wasn't a nice reply to a polite request. We'll ask a second time. Give us your daughter in marriage."

"I should really ask all her great grandmothers and great grandfathers for their permission. Will you wait while I do that?"

Cai frowned and turned to look at the others, and at that moment the Giant snatched up the second stone spear and hurled it at them.

Quick as a flash, Menw caught it and flung it back. It stuck in the Giant's chest.

"OUCH!" the Giant roared. "That itches! Now when I go upstairs I'll have trouble breathing, and a nasty tight cough."

Cai glared. "This is the last time we'll ask you," he snapped. "Don't attack us again. Give us an answer."

The Giant roared. "Servants and rascals! Raise my eyelids right to the top so I can see these puny men properly!"

His servants heaved at the sticks.

The Giant's eyes burned like the sun at midday.

He snatched the third stone spear and hurled it at them. This time Culhwch was ready, and he caught it and flung it straight back and it stuck in the Giant's eye.

"OUCH!" the Giant roared. "That's sore! Now my eyes will water in the wind and I'll get nasty headaches at each new moon. Curse you and this spear and whoever made it."

"That's enough!" Cai snapped. "Give us your answer."

The Giant was silent. Then he said, "You. The one who wants to marry my daughter. Come forward."

Culhwch stepped across the wide empty pavement of the hall. A servant brought a chair.

"Sit there," the Giant said.

Culhwch sat. He felt very scared and alone.

The Giant's enormous head bent down towards him. "So. If you want to marry my daughter, you will have to promise to get every single thing I ask for. If you fail in even one quest, the marriage will never happen."

Culhwch nodded. "I promise," he said.

The Giant took an enormous breath. He sprawled back in his throne and grinned with slabs of yellow teeth. "Right," he said. "Pin back your ears. This is what I want."

12. The Impossible Tasks

"First there must be a wedding feast. I want the field outside my fortress cleared and ploughed and sown with wheat. That must be done in one night. Only Amaethon son of Don can be the ploughman.

"Only the two enchanted oxen called Peibaw and Nyniaw yoked together can pull the plough.

"The wheat has to grow and ripen before the sun rises the next day, then be cut down and baked into bread for the feast.

"Also, I once had nine jars of flaxseed but they got spilled and the wind blew all the seed away. I want every single tiny seed of flax to be found to fill up my nine empty jars, and it must be done in a single day. That flaxseed must be planted and sown, so that a veil for Olwen's head can be spun from the flax, and if even one seed is missing, there's no wedding. Got that?"

Culhwch nodded. "That's all easy for me," he said calmly, "even if you think it's hard."

The Giant scowled. "Oh really? Well if you get that, you won't get the rest.

"I want the cup of Llwyr which holds the best drink

in the world and the hamper of Gwyddno Long-Legs that holds the best food in the world. I want the harp of Teirtu that plays by itself to entertain me and the birds of Rhiannon to sing to me. Most of all, I want the Cauldron of Diwrnach King of Ireland. It's the biggest cauldron in the world, and we'll need it to boil the meat for the wedding guests."

Culhwch dusted a speck off his coat. "That's all easy for me," he said, "even if you think it's hard."

The Giant growled. "Well, even if you get that, you won't get this.

"I will need to be washed and shaved for the wedding. My beard is so stiff and strong it will take the blood of the Very Black Witch, daughter of the Very White Witch from the Valley of Grief in the Uplands of Hell to straighten out its tangles. Also, there is only one comb and one razor and pair of shears in the world that can shave me.

"Those three things are hidden between the ears of the magic boar, the terrible Twrch Trwyth. Once he was a king, and he was transformed into a boar for his evil deeds.

"He will never give them up without a fight. So you'll have to organise a great Hunt to track him down."

Culhwch folded his arms. "That's easy for me, though you think it's hard."

The Giant stared at him closely. "I don't think you're as

cocky as you pretend. This is what you'll need to hunt the Twrch.

"Mabon, son of Modron, as the Huntsman. No one knows where he is. The two hounds called Aned and Aethlem, both as swift as the wind. The great dog called Drudwyn.

"There is no leash that can hold those dogs but a leash made from the beard of Dillus the Bearded, and the hairs must be plucked out while he is alive.

"There's no collar that can restrain those dogs but the collar of Canhastyr Hundred-hands.

"There's no horse fast enough to catch the Twrch but Myngddwn the steed of the Waves.

"There's no sword that can kill the Twrch but the sword of Wrnach the Enormous. He won't give it to you, so you'll never get it. All these things you'll need to hunt the great boar."

Culhwch swallowed. He whispered, "That's easy for me, though you think it's hard."

The Giant barked with laughter. "HA! I don't think so! I want all these things and you've got no chance of getting them, even if you lie awake at night plotting and planning for a hundred years. So you'll never marry my daughter."

Culhwch stood. He felt bewildered by all the tasks and names and objects. But then out of the corner of his eye he saw Olwen. She was standing under the arch of the hall, watching him, and she smiled and nodded, and yet she looked so sad that it made him angry. So he summoned up all his courage and swagger.

"I'll get everything you want. I have horses and horsemen and Arthur, the great lord of this Island, is my cousin, and his marvellous men and women will help me. And when I've got it all then I'll come back, and we'll hold the feast, and we'll shave you closer than you will like, and I will marry Olwen. And you, Giant, will die!"

He turned and strode out of the hall.

Cai and the others turned and strode out after him.

The Giant had no more spears left to throw. Only his laughter followed them down the corridors.

13. The Sword of Wrnach

They got on their horses and set out to ride back to Arthur's Court, but they were all very quiet and thoughtful.

At long last Culhwch sighed. "What a list of tasks! I can't remember half of it! Where do we even start!"

"I can remember them," Menw said quietly. "But they are many."

Cai looked ahead at the darkening sky, at the hills and valleys beyond, sinking into shadow. "We go back to Arthur's Court and we make a list and we make plans. It may not be impossible. Don't give up hope, Prince."

But Culhwch couldn't help feeling that the Giant had been too clever for them. How could he obtain all those swords and cauldrons and dogs and leashes and horns and combs – let alone hunt the terrible Twrch Trwyth! He felt thoroughly gloomy. Now he would never be able to marry Olwen.

The brief talk he had had with her had only inflamed his love.

It had been sickening to leave her behind, alone, in that dark fortress.

They rode for a long time. By nightfall they realised they were lost. Snow started to fall.

The land was dark and silent. The stars glittered in the sky.

Then, ahead of them on the ridge of a mountain, they saw an icy castle shimmering through the snowfall. A black-haired man came out of it and walked towards them. "Hey! You!" Cai shouted. "Whose castle is that?"

The man stopped and stared. "Are you stupid? Everyone knows that's the castle of Wrnach the Enormous."

"I'm getting really tired of being called stupid," Cai snarled.

Culhwch said, "Wait a minute! Wrnach the Enormous! He was on the Giant's list. He's the one that owns the sword, the only sword in the world that will kill the terrible Twrch! This is our chance to get it!"

Gwalchmai nodded. "Listen," he said to the black-haired man. "Do they allow guests and strangers in that castle?"

"No," the man said shortly. "It's too late at night. Knife has gone into meat and drink into horn and a throng is in the hall. The only person Wrnach might allow in is a craftsman."

"A craftsman?"

"Yes. A smith perhaps, or a musician."

Cai said at once, "Well that's me. I have a craft. I'm the best Polisher of Swords in the World."

The gatekeeper went in and found Wrnach the Enormous sitting at his high table with all his noisy, drunken, laughing warriors around him. "There's a band of men at the gate asking to come in. One of them says he's the best Polisher of Swords in the world."

"Is he now?" Wrnach growled. "Well that's useful. I've been looking for someone to polish my sword for some time. It's so magical I won't let it out of my sight. Let that man in."

The gatekeeper went back and let Cai in.

Cain marched up the hall and faced Wrnach, and almost laughed, because Wrnach the Enormous was clearly a jokey nickname. In fact Wrnach was a very tiny man, but he had a loud voice. He slurred, "Is it true, you can polish swords?"

Cai grinned. "You'll never see it shinier. I promise you."

Wrnach nodded. A servant came and lifted the precious sword from the table where it lay, and brought it to Cai. The sword was certainly big enough! As soon as Cai gripped it with his cold hands he could feel the magic pulsing in its steel and blade. He took a whetstone from his pocket. "Do you want it white-shiny or blue-shiny?"

"Whichever you like. Clean it as if it was yours."

Cai chose white-shiny. He polished half the blade and

gave it back. "How's that?"

"This is amazing work!" Wrnach held up the gleaming blade. "You're a fine craftsman. It's a shame a man like you has no companions."

"Ah but I do have a companion. He can throw a spear, so that the head of the spear comes off, draws blood from the wind, and then reattaches itself. He's called Bedwyr. There are others with him, equally handy."

The gatekeeper went out and let the others in, and they spread out inside the hall. Culhwch stared around, and saw most of Wrnach's men were drunk. Still, he knew there was only one way they would get out of here. By fighting.

Cai finished polishing the sword and held it up.

Every eye in the hall was drawn to it. Its glittering power dazzled them all.

"There! Finished." Cai stood up and came close to Wrnach. "Why don't you give me the leather sheath, because that's damaging your blade, and I'll fix that next." Wrnach tugged the sheath from his belt and held it out and Cai took it. He had the sword in one hand and the sheath in the other. Then he struck.

He took off Wrnach's head with one blow. The hall erupted into fury.

An hour later and many miles away, Cai drew his horse to a breathless halt and looked round. "Are we all here? Was anyone wounded?"

"We're all here," Menw said. "But it was a hard fight."

Gwalchmai nodded. "Lucky that most of them were drunk." Cwlhwch shivered. He had fought well, but now he was tired.

Cai laughed his cool laugh. He held up the Sword of Wrnach and it glittered in the icy starlight. "It was indeed. But look! One of the Giant's Tasks is completed. Even before we've got home!"

14. The Oldest Animals

"Well done, all of you," Arthur said, after hearing the full story. "But it seems we have a great deal of work to do."

"How can we achieve all those tasks?" Culhwch said gloomily. "There are so many..."

Arthur put an arm round his shoulders. "Don't you worry. I have the best warriors and wise-women here. Many of the things on the Giant's list I already know about, and they can be brought to me. Olwen and you will be married. I promised to get what you asked me and I will. So, where do we start?"

Gwenhwyfar said, "I think you should start by looking for the Huntsman, Mabon, son of Modron, because he will be the hardest of all to find. Do you know his story, Prince?"

Culhwch shook his head.

Gwenhwyfar smiled sadly. She said, "Mabon is the son of Modron, a great queen. He was stolen when he was three days old, lying in his bed between his mother and the wall. No one has seen him since. That was years ago. He'll be a young man by now. If he's still alive."

Arthur nodded. "Perhaps the Giant knows more than

we do. Cai, you'll lead the search. Bedwyr, and Prince Culhwch will go with you. And Gwrhyr All-Tongues, too, because I have a strange feeling we're going to need his skills for this."

"Where do we look?" Cai growled.

Arthur gazed out of the window of his hall. "Out there in wild Wales. Where you can find all the marvels of the world. Take my advice. Ask the oldest animals."

They set out and rode for seven days until they came to where the Blackbird of Cilgwri was perched on a branch.

Gwrhyr looked up and spoke to her. "Listen, Blackbird. We are messengers from Arthur. Do you know where we can find Mabon, son of Modron, who was stolen at three days old from between his mother and the wall?"

The Blackbird said:

I came here a tiny fledgling.
I perched on an iron anvil.
Every evening I sharpen my beak on it.
Through the centuries
It has worn away to the size of a nut.
In all that time
I have never heard of
The man you seek.

BUT!
There is an animal older than me.

The Blackbird took them to the Stag of Rhedynfre.

Gwrhyr spoke to him. "Listen, Stag. We are messengers from Arthur. Do you know where we can find Mabon, son of Modron, who was stolen at three days old from between his mother and the wall?"

The Stag said:

I came here as a youngster.
I had only two antlers then.
A single oak sapling
Stood in the valley.
That oak grew huge,
Grew a hundred branches,
Grew old and died.
In all that time
I have never heard of
The man you seek.

BUT!
There is an animal older than me.

The Stag took them to see the Owl of Cwm Cawlwyd.

Gwrhyr said to her, "Listen, Owl. We are Arthur's messengers. Do you know where we can find Mabon, son of Modron, who was stolen at three days old from between his mother and the wall?"

The Owl said:

I came here as a chick.
The valley was deeply wooded.
Men came and cut the trees.
A second wood grew,
That too was cut.
This is the third wood
My eyes have seen.
I'm so old my wings
Are stumps.
In all that time
I've never heard of
The man you seek.

BUT!
There is an animal older than me.

The Owl took them to the Eagle of Gwernabwy.

Gwrhyr said to him, "Listen, Eagle. We are messengers from Arthur. Do you know where we can find Mabon, son of Modron, who was stolen at three days old from between his mother and the wall?"

The Eagle said:

I came here as an eaglet.
Every night
From a rock
On the mountaintop
I peck at the stars.
Now it's worn to a stone
Smaller than your hand.
In all that time
I have never heard
Of the man you seek.

BUT!

Once I went to Llyn Llyw.
I sank my claws in a Salmon
He was so huge
He pulled me underwater!
When I escaped
I sent an army of eagles.
He formed squadrons of salmon.
We were all set for war.
But instead we made peace.
I did him a favour,
Pulled fifty spears out of his back.

He's the Oldest of All.
If he doesn't know where Mabon is,
No one does.

The Eagle took them on its wings and flew with them, over hills and farms and mountains until they came to Llyn Llyw, in the estuary of the river Hafren.

From this height the water was silver-brown and cold, and Culhwch could see the great Salmon, rippling under the surface, looking up at them.

They landed and climbed down.

The Salmon swam to the bank and put its head out of the water.

"Salmon," the Eagle said. "I've brought Arthur's messengers. They are looking for Mabon, son of Modron, who was stolen at three days old from between his mother and the wall. Can you help?"

The Salmon flipped its tail. "Yes. At least, I know where he is. You see, I often swim in the river Hafren. When the flood tide comes I ride its great wave up and up for miles until I come to the Shining Fortress of Caerloyw. Once I heard a man lamenting in that house of stone, crying out and sighing. Never had I heard such sadness! I swam right in beneath the wall, and called out, "Who are you in there, and what's the matter?"

A voice answered. "My name is Mabon ap Modron, and

I am here in the worst prison in the world. No one is as miserable as me!"

"Who keeps you prisoner?"

"I don't know! I've never seen them, but I think they are a group of witches."

"So how can you be rescued? By paying a ransom?"

"No. Only by attacking the castle. But it's impossible, you'll need an army of great warriors."

The Salmon looked at Cai. "I swam away then. And that's all I know."

Cai laughed. "Excellent! Because I know just where we can find that army!"

The Eagle flew them swiftly back to Arthur's court, and as soon as Arthur heard the story he gathered his armies of wild and strange warriors.

They marched to Caerloyw, and Culhwch went with them.

The Shining Fortress glittered like quartz in the sunlight, and beside it the river Hafren was deep and brown-silver and mysterious, its tide surging upstream.

"Now" Arthur cried. "*Attack!*"

The army crashed against the fortress walls. Arrows flew, swords clashed. The guards inside came pouring out in dark, shadowy armour. Culhwch had never seen such fighting as on that day.

But really, of course, the attack was only a pretence. It was just meant to create a diversion.

Because Cai and Bedwyr were not there, they were riding on the shoulders of the Salmon, up the tidal rush of the river, speeding on its wild wave, around the bends and over the weirs, splashed and soaked and breathless, until they glided right under the walls of the fortress, and the sound of the fighting was loud from beyond the gates.

Cai took out a hammer. With all their strength he and Bedwyr smashed and crashed it against the wall until the bricks cracked and the mortar crumbled and the stones fell into the water.

When the crack was big enough Cai climbed in.

Moments later he came back. He was carrying a young man, pale, starved, his chains broken, blinking in the sunlight.

Mabon, son of Modron!

They climbed down, and sat on the Salmon's back, and with a flick of its tail it sped away, downstream, towards the sea.

Cai wiped foam from his face and grinned at Bedwyr. "Another task completed" he said, with satisfaction.

15. The Last Lame Ant

Arthur's people were out all over the Island of the Mighty hunting for the things the Giant had demanded.

"Let's see how we're doing." Gwenhwyfar looked at her list. "We've got Mabon now to lead the hunt. He's been eating and drinking non-stop – he looks so much stronger! Arthur has been to Aberdaugleddau and found the two hounds, Aed and Aethlem. They are extremely ferocious."

Culhwch nodded. He had heard how the hounds had been found killing sheep there, and Arthur had sailed in his ship *Prydwen* to fetch them away.

"The dog Drudwyn has been given to us as a gift by Gwyn ap Nudd."

Culhwch nodded again. Arthur had made peace between Gwyn and his enemy Gwythyr, and had asked for the dog as his reward.

"Canhastyr Hundred-hands has brought the collar to hold the hounds," Gwenhwyfar went on." And yesterday, Myngddwn, the Horse of the Waves, trotted into the Court on his own and said he had heard about the Quest and had come to offer his services!"

Cai laughed. Sitting on the windowsill of the warm

room he said, "I wish they were all that easy!"

"So do I!" Gwenhwyfar said. She smiled at Culhwch. "Also, Rhiannon has sent her three magical birds to sing for the wedding, and Teirtu has sent her harp that plays by itself. The Hamper and the Cup already belong to members of the Court. But there are still some very difficult things. How can we get the beard of Dillus the Bearded or the blood of the Very Black Witch from the Uplands of Hell?"

"And don't forget the nine jars that have to be re-filled with flax seed without losing even one seed," Arthur murmured, his feet on the table. "That might seem a small task, but it's quite impossible."

"Actually, Lord," a voice said from the doorway. "It's not." They all looked up.

One of the warriors, the man called Gwythyr, was standing in the door. He looked tired and dirty and there was a small satchel on his back.

He came in, poured some wine and drank it off as if he hadn't drunk for days. "I have such a story to tell you," he said.

Arthur swivelled his feet down and leaned forward. "Go on."

"I was travelling over a mountain two days ago," Gwythyr began. "The sun had been very hot all day. As I came over the ridge I saw to my horror that the mountain was on fire. Flames crackled through the bracken and crisped the leaves of the rowan trees.

I turned my horse, ready to gallop to safety, when suddenly I heard voices. Hundreds of them. Tiny shrill *insect* voices, weeping and wailing, a terrible uproar! I dismounted and looked down and I saw an anthill, with millions of ants swarming in panic because of the fire, trying to carry their Queen and all her eggs away.

Well, I got out my sword and slashed the anthill off at the level of the ground and carried it away on my shield. I took it to the river and put it down on the bank there, where it would be safe from the fire.

The Queen Ant came out and spoke to me. She said, *"Arthur's warrior, take our blessing with you, and my greetings to your Lord. If there is anything you need, which no man can bring, tell me now, and my people will fetch it for you. Because you've saved us all."*

"Well, as you can imagine I thought about our tasks, and suddenly it was clear to me what the ants could help with..."

"Finding the flaxseeds!" Culhwch gasped.

"Exactly, Prince. I explained to the Queen what had to be done. The ants set off at once. They scoured every field and furrow, every ditch and drain, every ridge and reen, every wood and warren. Meanwhile, I rode hard for the Giant's fortress and the shepherd's wife brought out the nine empty jars for me. She was so excited!

"When I got back with them the ants had begun to arrive. You should have seen that sight! A long, winding line of ants, millions and millions of them, tiny and patient, and each one carrying a single seed of flax. They must have scoured the world to find them all."

Arthur smiled. "You did well," he said.

Gwythyr shrugged. "They did it. For hours they came in, and we filled all the nine jars until, at a minute to midnight, the last jar was almost full. Almost. Because there was space for just one more seed. And you know the Giant said if even one was missing, the task was a failure. I was ready to despair. But the Queen Ant said, *"Wait. Not all my people are here."*

"Then, just before the stroke of midnight, very slowly up the lane, limped the last lame ant. He couldn't walk as fast as the others, but he was just as determined, and he carried the final flaxseed and climbed up and dropped it into the jar. The nine jars were full!"

"That Queen and her people are part of my Court now!" Arthur leapt up "We must start the ploughing..."

"It's done, Lord." Gwythyr looked modest. "I got Amaethon son of Don to come and plough the field at once, with the two oxen, who both complained loudly all the time of being disturbed so late at night. The wheat was sown for bread, and the flax was sown and it grew up immediately and was harvested by me and the shepherd

Custennin. Elin his wife took it and shredded the stems and set up her wheel and spun the finest linen from the flax. She spun it in starlight and starlight is within it. She made the veil for Olwen to wear at her wedding. And here it is!"

He drew the veil from his bag and held it up. The fine fabric shimmered with the light of distant galaxies. Pearls hung from it like stars. Culhwch stared in wonder. "It's beautiful!" he whispered. "And Olwen will look even lovelier when she wears it." Arthur nodded. "So the smallest creature is no less powerful, in its way, than the greatest," he murmured. "We should always remember that."

16. Dillus the Bearded

Two days later, Cai and Bedwyr were sitting on top of Pumlumon cooking slivers of meat over a fire. They had ridden all afternoon and not found anything to help with the Tasks, and Cai was annoyed. Also it was cold and windy on the mountaintop.

They were sitting in the highest wind in the world. Suddenly Bedwyr said, "What's that?"

"Where?"

"There. It looks like another fire."

Cai looked with his sharp eyes. "It is a fire. And the strange thing is that the smoke is going straight up into the sky, and not being blown about by the wind. That's the fire of some magical evil being. Let's go and see who it is."

They crept and crawled nearer and got close enough to see a big man with a thick black beard sitting by the fire roasting a whole boar on a spit. The fat dripped and crackled in the flames, and the delicious smell made Bedwyr's mouth water.

"Do you know who he is?" he whispered.

Cai nodded. "I do. That is Dillus the Bearded. Remember the Tasks? The only leash in the world that can hold Drudwyn the Dog has to be made from his beard. And it has to be plucked out with wooden tweezers while he's still alive."

Bedwyr was worried. "How can we do that?"

Cai wore his most reckless look. "Leave him to eat and drink until he falls asleep. Then we move in."

While the man ate, Bedwyr made a pair of wooden tweezers. But as soon as the snores from the campsite told them Dillus was soundly asleep they stood up and walked in closer. Cai nudged Dillus with his foot.

"Dead drunk." He grinned. "Excellent."

Cai took a spade from his horse and began to dig. He dug a deep narrow pit and rolled Dillus into it, upright, and filled in the earth and trampled it down so that only the man's sleeping head remained above ground.

"Tweezers," he said. Bedwyr handed them over.

Cai crouched and plucked out a hair from the bristly black beard. Dillus gave a yell of pain and his eyes snapped open. He wriggled and struggled.

But he was buried deep.

Swiftly Cai plucked strand after strand of the beard and gave them to Bedwyr, who was already weaving and plaiting them into a leash.

But the huge man's struggles were causing earthquakes and tremors. The whole mountaintop was shaking. "When I get out of here," he roared, "you are

DEAD!" Cai kept plucking. Suddenly Dillus roared out and one arm came free. Then the other.

"Look out!" Bedwyr leapt back.

"Do we have enough?" Cai snapped.

"Yes! Yes! Plenty!"

"Good. Then he doesn't have to stay alive any more." Cai stood up. With one slice of his sword he took off the man's head.

Then he turned and walked away.

Bedwyr walked after him, casting one look back at the fire and the pit.

He shook his head. There were times when Cai was more terrifying than anyone.

When Arthur heard the story and saw the leash made of the beard he couldn't stop laughing. He thought the whole adventure sounded so ridiculous that he made a small poem about it and sang it.

Cai made a leash
From the beard of Dillus ap Efrai.
If he was alive, he'd kill you for it.

Cai folded his arms. His face was dark with fury. He stalked off, without saying a word.

Gwynhwyfar watched him go. "I think, my Lord," she said thoughtfully, "that you may have just made a big mistake."

It was then that Cai left the court and went off to his own fortress for a while. Arthur said to Culhwch, "Don't worry. I will find the next things myself. We can manage without my foster-brother."

Culhwch was not so sure.

That night he dreamed of Olwen, dressed in a dark cloak, wandering the cold stone corridors of the Biggest Fortress in the World, lonely and worried.

"Don't worry. I'm coming back," he whispered.

In his dream she looked up, as if she heard him.

17. The Irishman's Cauldron

The messenger stood wearily before Arthur's Court. All the champions and warriors and women looked at him in expectation. He had just come back from Ireland. "Well?" Arthur demanded.

"The King of Ireland, Diwrnach, sends you this reply to your message, Lord. He's not giving up his Cauldron to you. It's his most precious possession. He says, 'If you want it you'll have to come and get it.'"

Arthur stood up.

All his men stood too. "Let's go," he said.

On the ship called *Prydwen* Culhwch watched as the green shores of Ireland drew near. He wished that Cai was with them. He wished he wasn't giving Arthur all this trouble. But every time he thought of Olwen and her grim life in the empty fortress of the Giant, he knew there was nothing else he could do.

Arthur had brought only twenty men on this trip, including a huge man called Hygwydd whose usual job it was to carry Arthur's own cauldron on his back. They left the ship

and walked to the house of Diwrnach, a square thatched house with horses and stables and dogs and chariots littered around it.

Firelight and singing came from inside the house.

Arthur ducked under the low doorway and marched in. His men followed him. They sat down at the tables and looked round.

The Irish King knew at once who they were.

He frowned, but said nothing, only making a sign that they should have food and drink. As the food was served, Culhwch looked around, and drew a breath in wonder. In the centre of the hall was the Cauldron. It was truly enormous, hanging over the fire by three silver chains from the roof. Red and green enamel spirals decorated its rim. Smoke rose from it and delicious meaty cooking smells.

The stew was ladled out and brought and put on the tables in pewter dishes, and the men, who were tired from rowing, ate quickly.

Culhwch could only sip at some wine. His throat felt dry with nerves.

The fire crackled. Then Culhwch started to notice something else. The Irish bards, the druids, the priests, the children were all quietly leaving the hall. Some of the women stayed, but only those that wore swords. The Irish warband each had a spear and a sword, and they weren't eating now. They were watching Arthur's men. Silence fell.

Diwrnach stood up. "I know what you've come for, Arthur."

"Then give it to me now, without any bloodshed," Arthur snapped.

Diwrnach shook his head, stubborn. "Never. That's no ordinary cauldron."

"Which is why we need it." Arthur stood. "I don't want to fight you, but..."

It was too late. With a roar the Irish warriors had already attacked. Swords flashed.

Benches toppled.

Spears flew.

In all the chaos Bedwyr shoved and pushed his way to the fire and slashed the chains that held the Cauldron. With his silver hand he grabbed it and heaved it onto the back of the big man, Hygwydd.

"Run!" he yelled. "RUN!"

Hygwydd was the only man who could even have stood up with that weight on his back. He set off for the ships, and Arthur and his men came after him, fighting backwards all the way, and the path from the houses to the shore was littered with fallen men.

They all piled into the ship and set off home, breathless and sore.

When they were safely out to sea, Culhwch looked into the Cauldron, and frowned, puzzled. There was no stew.

Instead it was full of treasure, crosses and caskets and cups of gold and silver, interlaced with patterns and whirls and triskeles.

His eyes widened.

All the way back to the Island of the Mighty he sat with his arm around the Cauldron, thinking of Olwen.

18. Spying

Menw the Sorcerer flicked a wing,
preened a feather with his beak.
Jackdaw-black, glossy,
he hid among the holly.

Find the Boar, Arthur had said,
the terrible Twrch.
We need to know where he is,
the Hunt's nearly ready.

Menw the Sorcerer peered down,
his eye jackdaw-bright.
A rustle in the rushes.
Sharp bristles. A snout.

Boar once a king,
now snorting, rooting.
Between muddy ears,
Comb. Razor. Shears.

Menw the Sorcerer held his breath.
If he could snatch them now!

But as he hopped close the
Twrch shook his chops.

Saliva hung.
Poison flew.
Spattered Menw.
How it stung!

Flying home he moaned.
Magic had seared him.
He would always burn
with that sweet venom.

19. The Uplands of Hell

"Well the time's come!" Arthur said. "We need to set off to find the Very Black Witch, daughter of the Very White Witch in the Valley of Grief in the Uplands of Hell."

He looked round at his bold, adventurous men and women. No one jumped up and grabbed their weapons.

Nobody moved.

In fact none of them looked at all enthusiastic.

"Remind me," Gwalchmai said quietly, "why do we have to find her?"

"Because only her blood can untangle the Giant's beard before it can be shaved for the wedding," Culhwch said.

"Ah yes."

Everyone was silent.

No one liked the sound of the Uplands of Hell. Not for the first time, Culhwch wished Cai was here. Cai was always ready for danger.

It was Bedwyr who finally stood up. "Well," he said wearily, "we'd better get going. That blood is not going to fetch itself."

Arthur picked a carefully chosen warband for this one.

He took Gwyn son of Nudd, who had magical powers, and Gwythyr son of Greidol because he'd done so well with the ants. He took two very big servants, Cacamwri and Hygwydd, because everyone knew the Witch was extremely strong. He took two tall skinny sisters, Amren and Eiddil. He took a hundred other warriors, all armed to the teeth.

It was a long cold journey to Hell, far in the Old North, among wastelands of ice and rock. Culhwch was nearly frozen by the time they got there, and the whole warband was crusted with snow and had ice in their beards. Their eyes were red rimmed and their fingers chilblained.

The horses were limping with weariness.

Finally they crossed the ice and came to a jagged cave in a high glassy mountainside.

Arthur looked up at the dark opening. "This looks like it." The warband sat silently.

Out of the cave came a low, mocking cackle.

The horses shuffled nervously. The men looked at each other. "Cacamwri and Hygwydd," Arthur said. "Go in there and fight the hag."

The two big brothers grinned. They looked bold and eager. They dismounted, pulled out swords and knives and waded in.

There was a short silence.

Then came a huge roaring and crashing and shrieking and howling. Cacamwri was thrown out and landed on his head.

Hygwydd was tossed after him; he landed splat in the snow.

"Mmm," Arthur said. He looked annoyed. "All right. Tall Amren and Tall Eiddil. Get in that cave and sort out that witch."

The two skinny sisters grinned. They looked ready and willing. They stepped over the first two, pulled out swords and knives and waded in.

There was a short silence.

Then came a huge roaring and crashing and shrieking and howling. Tall Amren was hurled out and slid along the ice.

Tall Eiddil was flung after her and skidded into a snowdrift.

"What!" Arthur was furious. He began to dismount. "This is impossible! I'm going in myself...!"

"NO!" Everyone yelled it once. Then Gwyn ap Nudd said, "No, Lord! It wouldn't be right for you to be seen wrestling with a mere witch..."

"Then you go!" Arthur snapped. "And take Gwythyr with you!"

Gwyn and Gwythyr dismounted and took out swords and knives and spears and magic weapons. They looked anxious and uneasy.

They put down their heads and stormed the cave, screaming ferocious war cries. There was a moment's echoey silence.

Then came an ENORMOUS roaring and crashing and banging and shrieking and howling.

Gwythyr was hurled out on his back. Gwyn was flung on top of him.

"That's it!" Arthur snatched out his famous knife Carnwennan. "I'm not having this. Stand back."

Culhwch said "But Lord…"

Arthur took no notice. He gave Culhwch the reins of his horse and didn't shout or yell or run. He was ominously quiet. He walked steadily into the darkness of the cave.

The warband waited in the icy wind. They were deeply worried. There was a long silence.

And then a wail. An anguished cry so strange and eerie it made them all shiver and shudder where they sat.

Gwalchmai and Bedwyr leapt down, ready to rush in, but something moved in the darkness of the cave. They stood still, terrified that Arthur would be thrown out, maybe even dead.

Instead they caught a glint and a glimmer. Heard a slice and a spatter.

Arthur walked out of the darkness, breathless and worn, his hair streaked with sweat, his cloak bloody and his tunic torn by long nails.

He tossed a small sticky container up to his cousin, Caw of Prydyn. "Keep that safe," he said hoarsely. "It's some of the Witch's blood."

Culhwch stared at the dark mouth of the cave. So that was Hell!

He was very glad he hadn't been the one to go in.

The six wounded warriors had to be loaded onto the back of Arthur's horse Llamrei. They groaned and complained all the way home.

20. Twrch Trwyth

You out there!
Listen to my snarls.
Once I was a king.
The wickedest on earth.
No one could imagine
The darkness in my heart.
Darker than night
Or the space between stars.

It's going to take armies,
Even to approach me.
Going to take magic
To stop my rampage.
Going to take wonders
To pierce my skin.
Going to take guts
To steal my treasures.

I laugh at giants.
Scorn witches.
Eat warriors.
Chew druids.

I'm the last, the hardest,
the deadliest.
I'll tear up
Your land, your men,
Your hounds.
Arthur, in all the tales
For all the ages,
Our war will echo.

21. The Hunt Begins

So finally, at last, after months of work, everything was ready for the Hunt of the great Boar.

Mabon the Huntsman readied his dogs and hounds, held by their magic leash and collar. He rode his horse that ran faster than the waves.

Arthur gathered every warrior and druid in the Island of the Mighty. He sent for champions from France and Brittany and Normandy and the Land of Summer. The entire Court was mounted and armed. Thousands of men and women with strange magical powers rode out on the final quest – to find the Twrch Trwyth, and to take the comb and the shears and razor that lay between the ears of that mighty, evil king.

First they crossed the sea to Ireland, because Menw had told him that was where the Twrch was, together with his seven piglets.

When they landed in Ireland the people were so terrified at the size of the army that the saints of Ireland were sent to meet Arthur. They asked what was going on.

Arthur told them they were all safe. It was just the Twrch his army wanted. They looked very glad. "The

Twrch and his piglets are in a place called Esgair Oerfel," they said. "He's been there a week, and he's destroying everything in sight. Our army has been scared to go against him, but now we'll join up with yours."

So the armies came to Esgair. All the hounds were loosed against the Twrch, and the Irish army fought against him all day until the sun went down. They couldn't even make him sweat.

The next day Arthur's army fought him. They couldn't even scratch him.

On the third day Arthur put all his armour on and went and fought the Twrch and the piglets on his own. Their combat made the hills shake and the woods cower.

But at the end of it Arthur had only managed to kill a single piglet.

That night round the campfire, Arthur said to Gwyhyr All-Tongues, "Go and talk to him. Tell him we need the comb and the shears and the razor to shave the Giant for the wedding. Ask him to give them to me before this gets too serious."

Gwrhyr said to Menw, "You'd better change me into a bird. I want to be able to fly away fast!"

So, in a bird's shape, he flew to where the Twrch and the six piglets wallowed in the black mud of a slimy hollow.

Gwrhyr perched on a branch. "Twrch!" he whispered.

The boar-king raised his head. Mud and slime and blood dripped from his raw mouth.

His teeth were razors.

His bristles dripped poison. His breath was acid.

His eyes were dead.

He gave the bird one fearsome look and went back to his wallowing.

Gwrhyr didn't dare to come closer. Instead he spoke to the piglets. "Please, will one of you come and talk to Arthur? We just need your help."

The piglet called Grugyn Silver-Bristle raised his shiny head and snarled. "We won't do anything to help Arthur. We've been cursed by God, and doomed to this horrible shape for ever. And now Arthur wants to attack us too?"

"Arthur needs the comb and razor and shears that are between the Twrch's ears," Gwyhyr said, edging away nervously.

"We won't give them. We live in pain and darkness and we want revenge. The Twrch says tomorrow we leave here. We're going to Arthur's own land. And we'll tear it apart."

Gwrhyr opened his beak but at that moment the Twrch rose out of the swamp and gave such a roar he flew away in terror as fast as he could, all the way back to the Court.

Arthur heard the message with a grave face.

"So he's attacking us now, is he? Well this is where the

killing begins."

A horseman galloped into the camp. He swung down and pushed through the host of warriors into the circle of the fire, and the red light shimmered on his fair hair and sharp weapons.

He stopped opposite to Arthur and they stood eye to eye. "Not without me, brother," Cai said.

22. The Terrible Rampage

1. Dyfed

They went to their ships.

Twrch Trwyth and his pigs swam the sea and landed in Porth Clais. By the time the Hunt caught up the Twrch had killed all the cattle in Dyfed and was trampling the town of Aberdaugleddau.

Arthur's men rode fast but that afternoon the Twrch was already at Preseli, and by the time they got there all the sheep of Dyfed had been slaughtered too.

Arthur sent all his warband in, Mabon holding the two hounds and Drudwyn held by Gwyn ap Nudd. The Hunt spread out, hundreds wide, with Cai leading the right flank and Bedwyr the left, and Bedwyr had Cafall, Arthur's dog. They lined up on the banks of the river Nyfer and the dogs were loosed.

The Twrch crossed the river to Cwm Cerwyn, and there he turned and fought.

In that place he killed four of Arthur's men.

He backed off a little and turned and fought again, killing another four warriors. "But he's wounded," Cai said, that night, as the injured were tended.

"I saw his blood."

Next morning, the Hunt set out again. The Twrch killed the three servants of Glewlwyd Great-Grip. He killed Arthur's carpenter, Glwyddyn Saer, and many other warriors. The Hunt caught up with him near Narberth, and there he killed three more men. Then he raced to Aber Tywi, where he killed two others and then the mists rose over Glyn Ystun, and the men and hounds lost his scent.

That night Arthur sent for Gwyn ap Nudd, and Menw, and the druids and bards and those who knew magic. "Any suggestions?" he snapped.

"We're saying all the spells we know," Menw said. "But nothing works on him. He is cursed by God."

"He's killing too many of my men." Arthur growled.

Culhwch looked away. He wished there was something he could do.

Next day they hunted the piglets. They found Grugyn Silver-Bristle and Llwydog Gofyniad but those two killed a lot of men. Arthur came hurrying up and set all his hounds loose, and the barking and yelping and snorting were so loud the Twrch heard them and came to defend his piglets.

There was a terrible battle.

By the end of the day's fighting only two piglets were left. They were Grugyn and Llwydog.

Three days' chase followed, through the lakes and mountains, through the green vales of Dyfed. The piglets split up; Grugyn was chased into Ceredigion, and he was killed at Garth Grugyn, but not before more men were wounded. Llwydog was killed at Ystrad Yw, on a pile of bodies of Arthur's champions.

Then the news came in that the Twrch had turned east. He was rampaging his way through Gwent, down to the river Hafren.

"Now we've got him!" Arthur closed his fists. "Now we've got him," he muttered.

2. GWENT

As they rode Arthur was getting more and more angry.

"The Twrch is savage and we can't let him cross the river into Cornwall!"

"Then we ambush him at the river," Cai had said. "We'll drive him into the Hafren and kill him there."

Now the dogs and hunters were all waiting, spread out in a great line by the vast muddy brown-silver estuary. The hounds yelped and fought. The sun glinted in Culhwch's eyes. He was cold and shivering with excitement. Then he saw a flash of pale skin – a huge animal in the reens and reeds.

"There!" he yelled."There he is!"

The Twrch reared out of the mud, and stood at bay, his back to the huge tidal river. "Now!" Mabon yelled.

The Hunt attacked.

Every warrior in the Island,
Every wise woman, every druid,
Reeds and birds and fishes,
Wind and wave and worm.
This is the hour
That darkness is broken.
This is the hour
That Olwen is won.

The Twrch was driven and forced by the onrush right into the river.

Mabon, son of Modron, didn't stop. He spoke to the horse Myngddwn and it galloped into the water, and the hounds Aned and Aethlem and the dog Drudwyn followed, yelping and barking, and Culhwch, and Goreu son of Custennin, and Menw and Bedwyr and Gwenhwyfar and Cai.

This was in a place between Llyn Lliw and the estuary of the Wye.

It was here Arthur leapt from his horse onto the Twrch, and Osla Big-Knife was with him, and Gwalchmai, and Cacamwri. They grabbed the boar by his hooves and hauled him down, so that the tide swept him off his feet and flooded over him. He thrashed and roared. And Mabon spurred his wave-horse and leaned over and snatched the Razor, and on the other side Cai snatched the Shears. And Culhwch, with the last gasp of breath he had in him, bent down, his fingers stretching and stretching until he touched the small wet spines of the Comb. He snatched it up with a cry.

At that moment the Twrch's feet touched the sea bed.

He broke away and flung off his hunters with a mighty roar. He plunged into the tide and swam.

Towards Cornwall.

They had a lot of trouble pulling everyone out of the water. Cacamwri was so big it was like pulling out two millstones.

Osla's knife fell from its sheath and was lost, and the sheath filled up with water and pulled him down, so that he nearly drowned.

Culhwch felt his hand and arm had been pulled apart. Every bone was aching. But they had the treasures!

Arthur sent the three precious treasures back to Court, with Culhwch, Goreu the shepherd's son and an escort of mighty men to guard them.

Then he said, "The rest of us need to go to Cornwall. We can't have the Twrch destroying everything in revenge. Wait for us."

It was two weeks before the army limped back to Court.

That night bards told the story of the Hunt of the Twrch Trwyth, and of how Arthur had followed him down into Cornwall, over the moors and mires, and trapped him on the beach.

But there the Twrch had laughed, and entered the sea and swum away. And from that day to this, nobody knows where he went.

23. The Shaving of the Giant

In the great hall of Ysbaddaden Chief-Giant, black banners were hung. Sable curtains darkened the doors and windows.

Purple glossy velvet was worn by all the servants and rascals. Arthur's men and women, in bright silks, stood in a mighty crowd. A thousand candles flickered.

The Giant was a mountain of darkness on his throne.

He looked around at all the things he had demanded. The Cauldron of Diwrnach was boiling food. The harp of Teirtu and the birds of Rhiannon were making sweet music. The hall was full of food and dogs and horses and people and vats of drink.

Everything he had asked for was there.

Then Olwen came.

She wore white satin, and white flowers sprang up at her feet.

On her head was the linen veil woven from the flax, glittering with starlight, shimmering with pearls.

She stood beside Culhwch and they looked each other

in the eyes. "You did well," she said.

Culhwch nodded. "With the help of my friends. Are you ready to be free?"

Olwen looked at the Giant sadly. She said,
"The time has come.
The young must inherit from the old.
Daylight must win over darkness.
Death must come to all.
Love must flower in our footsteps."

The Giant glared back at her from his red-rimmed eyes. "I agree with you. Goodbye, my daughter," he said. "Bring up my grandchildren well." Then he roared, "Come and shave me, warriors!"

Caw son of Prydyn took the blood of the Witch and soaped the Giant's beard, and then he combed it with the Comb and trimmed it with the Shears and then he took the Razor and shaved Ysbaddaden Chief-Giant's beard off, right down to the bone. Culhwch said, "Have you been shaved, Giant?"

"I have."

"Can Olwen and I be married now?"

The Giant growled. "You can. But you have to admit you would never have been able to do it without Arthur's help. So now, let's get this over and done!"

But it wasn't Arthur who stepped forward, or Cai, or Bedwyr. It wasn't Menw or Gwythyr or Gwenhwyfar.

It wasn't any of the mighty magical heroes of the Court.

It was the small boy, Goreu, last son of the shepherd Custennin.

He carried the Sword of Wrnach the Enormous, and he said, "This is my duty, because the Giant killed all my twenty-two brothers and I am the Last and Best. So this is for them."

Goreu leapt up. He sliced off the Giant's head, and dragged it outside. He came back and sat on the throne, and took over the fortress and the land and the flocks of sheep for himself and his father Custennin and his mother, Elin.

Culhwch and Olwen were married with all ceremony. And the feast began.

24. Home

While all of Arthur's men were eating and drinking and singing, Olwen turned to Culhwch. Quietly she said, "You were born in a pig-run, and you won me by hunting the boar. How strange that is."

Culhwch smiled. "Tomorrow we go back home, and you will meet my father and his wife."

Olwen nodded. "And I'll place flowers on the grave of your mother, who began all this."

"To Goleuddydd," Culhwch said, lifting his wine glass.

Around him, all the hosts of Arthur stopped singing and eating and arguing and drinking. They raised their cups and horns and chalices.

"To Goleuddydd," they said, as the servants pulled down the dark hangings and the glorious sunlight poured in.

"To Daylight."

CATHERINE FISHER

Catherine Fisher is a *New York Times* best-selling author. Her novel *Incarceron* was the *Times* Children's Book of the Year, 2007. She has twice won the Tir na n-Og prize, and has been shortlisted for the Blue Peter, Carnegie, Costa and WHSmith prizes. She has published over 35 novels, translated into more than 40 languages, and is also a prize-winning poet.

EFA LOIS

Efa Lois is an experienced illustrator having produced work for Visit Wales, the National Library of Wales, Cadw, the Tafwyl festival and *Cara* magazine. Efa has also illustrated several Welsh-language titles including *Cymry o Fri* by Jon Gower and *Y Stori Orau* by Lleucu Roberts.